# A Welsh Woman's Reflections

# A Welsh Woman's Reflections

*by*

## BRENDA JONES

YOUCAXTON PUBLICATIONS
OXFORD & SHREWSBURY

www.brendajones.net
brenda54@hotmail.co.uk
01691 652067

Edited by
Mike Willmott
www.shrewsburywords.com
shrewsburywords@hotmail.com
01743 366933

Front cover design
Gerald Newton
newtongerald@yahoo.co.uk

ISBN 978-1-911175-32-2
Printed and bound in Great Britain.
Published by YouCaxton Publications 2016

TO ALL FRIENDS AND FAMILY

WHO HAVE PROVIDED ME WITH INSPIRATION

# INTRODUCTION

I HAVE NOW TRIED MY HAND at writing short stories, following the success of my first two books of poetry – 'A Welsh Woman's View' (sold out), 'A Welsh Woman's Miscellany', and a CD of my poems with harp music. This has resulted in this book - 'A Welsh Woman's Reflections'.

I hope you will enjoy reading this book as much as I have enjoyed writing it. It's been great fun. The ideas for these stories come from personal experience, a chance comment uttered by someone, a snippet of overheard conversation, an observation, etc.

Some of them are written from the heart, and I try to give them all an unusual ending, whenever possible. Any profits from this book will go to the Alzheimer's Society, towards research. So far, profits from my first two books and CDs have resulted in my being able to send £3,600 to the Alzheimer's Society, and £500 to Cancer Research. I don't make a personal profit from my books.

Many thanks must go to my Editor, Mike Willmott – his expertise in English grammar and punctuation is second to none.

Many thanks also to Illustrator Gerald Newton - his bright, colourful book covers always stand out on the book shelves.

Happy reading everyone!

**Brenda Jones, April 2016**

# EDITOR'S FOREWORD

IT HAS BEEN A PLEASURE to work with Brenda on her writings. We have come up with a good formula – 'editorial collaboration'. In the last analysis, these are all her own words, after some discussion about finer points of grammar and punctuation with me the old-fashioned pedant.

Whether she is writing poems, or short stories, or speaking in public places, she has a unique voice. She tells life as it is. Her subjects range from the bane of alcoholism, to the joys of the family, from weddings to funerals, from childhood to old age: life's rich tapestry.

Deep down, I think she is writing about a sense of security – of knowing where you are in what life throws at you. She has an ample supply of such a sense of personal and social security, buoyed up by a wonderful family, and friends. But she knows well the times when we all don't feel secure. And for those struggling with life's problems, she shows supreme tact and understanding. Also, her Welsh humour shines through, to make life bearable:

*Quote*: 'Roast beef and Yorkshire pudding,' she mused. 'That's certainly something to smile about.'

**Mike Willmott, April 2016**

# CONTENTS

# HOME ALONE

THE HOUSE WAS SO QUIET she could hear the embers of the fire sighing into ashes. How strange it felt to be alone! Usually, the house was a hive of activity. But tonight, she only had her own shadow for company. During the day, she felt fine, but as soon as daylight dwindled to welcome the darkness came a sense of foreboding. Sounds, that during the day seemed perfectly normal, suddenly took on a macabre ambience. She had enjoyed her day - being able to catch up with jobs that had been left - but now, she felt afraid. What was it about darkness that changed your train of thought? Was it fear of the unknown - the fact you couldn't see what was really there?

As she entered the house that evening a crowd of crows flapped into the air, like blackened scraps of paper billowing up from a bonfire. The sound had made her jump; she scolded her own stupidity. She sat in the darkness, and heard a mouse scuttle in the attic. The house creaked and rattled: the wind had increased. She switched on the television, but nothing appealed to her. Why couldn't she find a programme she liked? She wasn't difficult to please.

The outside sensor light suddenly shone. She got up to look through the window, but could see nothing unusual - perhaps it had been a cat, or even a rabbit? But the yard was devoid of any life form. So what had triggered the light? She had locked all the doors and windows; she was quite safe, so why did she feel uneasy? She had read somewhere, 'We are our own worst enemy,' and thought, how true this was. Too many stories about ghosts, poltergeists, large arachnids, and headless apparitions, perhaps? Pieces of furniture, which during the day looked like furniture, appeared menacing, seeming to hide whatever there was behind them, and whatever they contained. The shrill sound of the telephone made her start; the sound of her husband's voice calmed her troubled mind.

"Are you ok?" he asked.

"Of course!" she replied. She didn't want to worry him: she knew she was overreacting.

After some other pleasantries he said, "See you tomorrow."

"Yes," she replied, and returned the receiver to its cradle. She got ready for bed, still listening out for unusual sounds. She caught sight of herself in the bathroom mirror. She smiled, but the smile in her reflection didn't quite reach her eyes - it looked false. She picked up a book, hoping it would make her sleepy. It did.

Next morning, she awoke with the sun streaming in through her bedroom window. She got up happily: today, her husband was coming home. Last night's insecurities seemed a lifetime away. She got dressed quickly, and ran downstairs, excited at the prospect of a brand new day.

\*\*\*

# TOMORROW IS ANOTHER DAY

H E SAT STARING AT THE TELEVISION, but not really seeing it. On the small oak table to his left sat half a glass of whisky. He looked at it - it was tempting him. He raised the glass to his lips, and took a sip. The yellow liquid burned his throat, but he didn't feel it. He felt numb.

Why had he bought the whisky? That was a good question. He supposed things had been building up for some weeks – little things, nothing major, until he felt he couldn't cope. So, instead of voicing his thoughts and dealing with his problems, he'd decided to do what he always did - numb his senses instead. He'd done this more and more often in recent months. What he didn't seem to realise was, although the alcohol seemed to help him initially, it didn't help at all in the long run. All it did was make him angry, cloud his judgement, alienate everyone around him, and make him incapable of sorting out anything.

He'd met his friend for coffee earlier in the day, and had treated her appallingly. He'd blamed her for his problems, shouted at her, and told her their friendship was over. He had rung later to apologise, and told her it wasn't her fault. So, in his numbed state, he thought everything would be all right. He knew he'd behaved badly, but when he drank, good manners went out of the window. She was bound to forgive him, wasn't she? He didn't know for sure. She had in the past. Oh, why did he push everyone away? He'd lost so many friends. He always took his frustrations out on the people closest to him. The truth was, alcohol made

3

him selfish and thoughtless. He looked at his phone. Why hadn't she texted him? Perhaps she was angry. She'd certainly looked very sad when he'd left her in the café. He picked up his phone to text her, but in his drunken state, sent an empty text.

"Damn!" he said to himself, and tried again. "Sorry," he typed, and pressed 'Send'. She was bound to respond - she always did. She often said he was like Jekyll and Hyde, but he wasn't that bad, was he? He had no idea how much his harsh words hurt her. When she told him what he'd said to her, he didn't always believe her - thought she was exaggerating. But perhaps she wasn't. The truth was, he couldn't remember. His excuse would always be, 'Oh I was drunk.' But it was too late - the words had been uttered, the impact made. She'd often told him what a nice, caring person he was when sober, so why couldn't he remain like that? He stared at his phone, willing it to respond, telling him a text had come through. He knew it was the lies that upset her more than anything – the fact he denied he was drinking, when he actually was. She'd told him he was in denial – perhaps he was. Still nothing.

He wondered whether he had pushed her too far. Had she reached breaking-point? Everyone had one. What he didn't realise was, every time he drank, got angry, told lies, he was actually chipping away at their friendship. Soon, there would be nothing left. But he needed her. He needed someone who was on the outside, looking in - someone who could see things clearly, with an objective view.

Sometimes, when you are too close to a problem, you can't see the wood for the trees. He drained his glass, looked at his phone one last time, decided his friend wasn't going to respond that night, and thought he'd better get to bed. Things would look better in the morning, hopefully, and by then, she might have texted. He hoped so. After all, tomorrow, was another day.

# MOTHER AND SON

S HE FELT A SENSE OF LOSS: her son had got married that very day. She was being ridiculous, she told herself - his now wife - meant the world to her. But this was the end of a chapter - the little boy she loved so much had grown up. Where had the years gone?

Her thoughts returned to January 1982, when he was born. Snow had caused anxiety for many weeks, so it was just as well he was two weeks late - weighing in at 7lbs 13ozs. She remembered her grandmother's words when she came to visit at the hospital, "He's been here before!" She was to remember those words many times in later years. The nurses had fallen in love with her 'strawberry blonde' baby.

The day she brought him home was cold, but then, what else could one expect in January? Her husband had turned up the central heating, before collecting his wife and baby son from the hospital. One of the nurses had said, "I hope you have central heating!" This statement made her wonder what on earth people had done in years gone by - children had obviously survived. The air of confidence which enveloped her before the birth had now deserted her. She suspected her hormones were responsible for this change in attitude. She and her husband were parents - how would they cope?

She wasn't mentally prepared for the endless feeling of tiredness, made worse by the dreaded night-feeds. She hated being woken in the dead of night, by her baby's hungry cries. There was something decidedly eerie about being up and about in the early hours. Mercifully, this lasted only a few weeks - she could cope, if her sleep was undisturbed.

Playschool was a wrench, followed quickly by Junior School. Her son was older than his years; she remembered her grandmother's words. He seemed to go through his teenage years whilst at Junior School, and when he finally reached High School, he was already a grown man, in his mother's eyes.

Mother and son had a bond: he knew what she was thinking, and vice versa. She only had to start a sentence and he automatically knew what she was going to say. She would sit on the edge of his bed, late in the evening, and they would put the world to rights - precious mother-and-son moments. If she was annoyed about something, he would distract her - divert her attention. She realised what he was doing, and applauded his common sense - only in her mind, of course. She had a specific sense of humour: only her son could really make her laugh, but he could also make her cry. He was a realist - no time for sentiment, but that was a mask he wore for the outside world.

The wedding was an intimate affair, with only twenty-eight guests; it was emotional, due to the fact that the bride's grandmother's funeral had taken place two days before the wedding: bad timing - but these things happen. The service was short but beautiful, the speeches emotional - some funny. Her son's speech amazed her: he was mischievous, but serious. She was so proud of him. When did he achieve this ease of talking in public? Perhaps she had brought him up the right way after all? Babies don't come with a text book: you can only teach them right from wrong - the rest is up to them. She had done well. The whole day was family-orientated, the children having the time of their lives.

All too soon, it was time to leave. She hugged her son - a rare occurrence: he wasn't demonstrative, unlike his new bride. In the dimly-lit car her tears flowed freely - she didn't know why. Perhaps she was tired: it had been a long day. She recovered temporarily on reaching home, but in the darkness of her bedroom her tears flowed again. If someone had asked her why she was crying, she would have been unable to give them a reason. Perhaps she was afraid there would be no more mother-and-son moments - but of course there would! She also knew that, in the morning, she would feel quite differently.

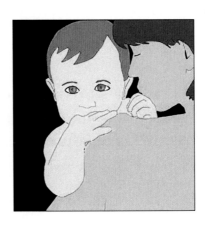

# APRIL FOOL

G RACE SAT IN HER LIVING ROOM, looking through the window at the snow falling erratically from the heavily-laden grey sky. She couldn't believe it – this time last week she had eaten her lunch outside on the newly-mown lawn, in soaring temperatures. She remembered wistfully the smell of the grass, and the sound of a bumble bee buzzing lazily from flower to flower.

It was the first of April – was God playing an April Fool? Grace recalled her childhood – in those days, snow came in winter, and the sun shone in summer: life was simple. Now, anything could happen. 'There must be at least eight inches of snow out there,' she thought.

It was the Easter school holidays, so the children living nearby were building a snowman. A good job they were making of it too – two stones for the eyes, a carrot for the nose, a pipe in its mouth, a bowler hat, scarf, and a walking stick. The snowman seemed to be smiling at Grace. She couldn't help but smile back – he looked so realistic. The children suddenly noticed her, and waved - she often watched them playing. They were always well behaved – 'Children get so much bad press these days,' thought Grace, but she never witnessed any bad behaviour.

Grace had lived alone since her husband Neil's death, six years before. Her son and daughter, and their families, lived locally, so she saw them regularly. She had four young grandchildren: she considered herself to be very lucky indeed.

Grace's thoughts returned to her childhood – she remembered not being able to attend Junior School for six weeks, because the road was blocked with snow: the snowploughs probably weren't as efficient then as they are now. She actually remembered walking on the river that meandered through her father's land – it was frozen solid. There had been a water leak in one of the fields – as a result, Grace had a ready-made skating rink. She had walked to the local village with her mother to buy essentials – it was the only way: the delivery van couldn't make the treacherous journey out into the countryside. Life was fun; she didn't remember feeling cold, although it must have been freezing. She used to sledge down a field, with only a wire fence to prevent her being catapulted into her father's garden, which would certainly have been frowned upon.

Suddenly, her reverie was interrupted – her four grandchildren burst into her kitchen.

"Hello, Nain!" they all shouted. Sophie, the eldest said, "We're just checking you're ok, and we've brought you some cake Mam baked this morning." Grace was thrilled to see them. Their faces glowed healthily after their hike through the snow. They kicked off their boots, and sat before the welcome fire to warm their toes – extremities were always the first to suffer in winter. They chatted happily – obviously pleased to be on holiday, and of course, the snow was an added bonus.

"Did you see the snowman?" Grace asked.

"Oh yes," answered Tomos, the youngest. "But he's not as good as ours. You must come and see him before he melts."

"I'll come tomorrow," said Grace. "I'm sure he'll last till then - they forecast frost for tonight." She made them four mugs of drinking chocolate, and opened a pack of chocolate biscuits. 'However did we manage before chocolate was discovered?' thought Grace.

Having been fed and watered, the children took their leave.

"You will come over for dinner tomorrow, won't you, Nain?" asked Gemma and Glyn, the twins. "We're having roast beef, Yorkshire pudding, and trifle for dessert."

"Oh lovely! How could I resist!" replied Grace. "I'll be with you by twelve noon."

"Great!" enthused all four. "We'll come and meet you. Bye!" Grace watched them go. When they were almost out of sight, they turned and waved, then were gone.

Grace felt uplifted by their visit – such energy and enthusiasm. She turned to pick up the empty mugs, and what remained of the biscuits. 'Roast beef and Yorkshire pudding,' she mused. 'That's certainly something to smile about.'

# IRIS

Iris sat in a room she didn't recognise. She couldn't remember how she'd got there, but the room was warm, light, and spacious, with a television in the corner. The *This Morning* programme was on - she recognised Phillip Schofield – or at least the voice seemed familiar. There were a number of people sitting in the room with her, but she didn't recognise any of them. Some were asleep, others chatting noisily – too noisily, Iris thought. A young girl wearing a white tunic and black trousers brought her a cup of tea.

"Here you are, Iris," she said. "Don't let it get cold." Iris picked up her cup, and took a sip. She pulled a face - they'd put sugar in it. She hadn't taken sugar in her tea for years.

Iris must have fallen asleep, because the next thing she knew, someone was patting her hand. She looked up – it was the girl in the white tunic again.

"Wake up, Iris, Sarah's here," she said, and when Iris looked vague, she added, "Your daughter's come to see you."

"Hello, Mam," said a voice she knew.

"Hello, Cariad," replied Iris, and looked up at her visitor, but was disappointed - she didn't recognise her. Why had her visitor got her daughter's voice, when it wasn't her? She felt so confused - she knew she'd had a daughter once; she could visualise her playing when she was a little girl. She had been a beautiful child - everyone said so. Iris wondered where her child was now.

"How are you, Mam?" asked Sarah. Iris just stared at her visitor, and thought perhaps she should answer, to avoid being rude.

"I'm ok," she replied.

"Emma and Tom send their love," said Sarah, and when Iris didn't respond, Sarah explained, "Your grandchildren, remember?" She had grandchildren? Iris couldn't remember them at all. Sarah smiled at her mother. "Never mind, Mam, I'll bring them with me next time - they might jog your memory."

All of a sudden, Iris asked, "Where's Mike?" Sarah immediately looked sad.

"Dad died two years ago, Mam," she replied. Iris was stunned: they'd only just got married, surely? She remembered the day so clearly. She'd worn an ivory wedding dress, with a shoulder-length veil, satin shoes, and a bouquet of burgundy and white roses. Mike had looked resplendent in a black suit, white shirt, with burgundy waistcoat and cravat. Sarah's voice interrupted her reverie:

"I'll have to go, Mam - the children will be home from school. I'll come and see you again very soon." Sarah kissed her mother on the cheek, and turned to leave. Iris watched her walk away, turn to wave - and then she was gone. She raised her hand to return the wave, but was too late. She wondered if she'd been dreaming - had her daughter really been to visit her? Everything was so confusing – she could remember her own childhood clearly, but everything else seemed to be shrouded in a dense fog. A tear meandered down her cheek. What was happening to her?

"Wasn't it nice to see Sarah?" The girl in the white tunic was back - she had a badge with 'Paula' written on it. "Come along, Iris, take my arm - it's time for tea. We have salmon sandwiches, trifle, and chocolate cake today." Paula helped Iris to her feet, and walked slowly with her into the dining room. Iris suddenly realised she was hungry, and Paula's description of the menu made her mouth water.

While Iris was eating, her thoughts returned to her visitor. She hoped it wouldn't be too long before Sarah came back to see her – she longed to hear her daughter's voice again.

# GUARDIAN ANGEL

DAVID WAS WALKING HOME across the fields, after spending the previous night with his friend Ben. They'd had such fun watching a ghostly DVD, and being scared out of their wits. To add to their pleasure, they'd woken up in the morning to find everything covered in six inches of snow. They'd spent the day building a snowman, sledging, and having snowball fights – all things ten-year-old boys love.

David's house was only three fields away from Ben's, so David was taking this route, rather than going by road, which would have taken him much longer. The snow was almost up to the top of David's wellies, so he was trying to be careful of his footing. He didn't want snow in his wellies - his feet were cold enough as it was.

It was late afternoon, but David had plenty of time to get home before darkness descended. As he trudged along, he noticed clouds gathering overhead, and a few snowflakes danced playfully on his face. 'If it snows again tonight, perhaps the school bus won't come tomorrow,' thought David, hopefully. Very quickly, the few snowflakes became a storm, until David found himself at the centre of a whirling blizzard. He battled against the wind, which had arisen from nowhere. He hoped he was going in the right direction: he could see his house before, but now he had no idea where it was. 'I mustn't panic,' he thought to himself, but he really wasn't sure if he was going the right way. He thought of his parents, his younger sister and ageing granddad, sitting in their warm farmhouse kitchen – he wished he was there.

All of a sudden, someone grabbed his arm.

"Granddad!" said David, relieved that someone had come to meet him.

"Just as well I came," said Granddad. "You're veering off in the wrong direction."

"How can you tell which way to go?" asked David.

"Experience - and years of walking these fields," replied Granddad.

In a short while, to David's immense relief, he saw a light – it was the sensor light that came on automatically when anyone entered the farmyard.

"You go indoors - I'll check on the dogs," said Granddad. David walked up the steps, and into the warm kitchen.

"Thank goodness!" said David's mum, relieved. "We were just coming to look for you. I tried ringing Ben, but the telephone lines must be down."

"It was quite scary," replied David. "I was going the wrong way until Granddad found me, and brought me home."

Everything went quiet.

"What?" asked David. David's mum came towards him. "We have some very bad news," she said. "I'm so sorry, David, but Granddad died last night."

"But I've just seen him! He's gone to check on the dogs," said David, tears coming involuntarily down his face.

David's dad smiled. "It seems Granddad is still looking out for you: he must be your guardian angel."

***

# KNIGHT IN SHINING ARMOUR

MARIA FELT A SHIVER run down her spine. She suspected she was being followed - she could hear footsteps. Intuition told her it was a man. Maria stopped to listen - nothing. She continued - there it was again. Maria had only moved into the village a week before, so she was still unsure of her surroundings. To make matters worse, fog had descended from nowhere: she wasn't sure where she was. It was still light when she left her friend Elaine's cottage, and the darkness was premature - brought on by the fog, no doubt. Maria accelerated her step - so did her pursuer. Don't panic, she thought - it might be your imagination: think rationally. But at times like this, the last thing you feel is rational. Beads of perspiration appeared on her body, even though the fog was cold. Her throat felt dry - she couldn't shout for help, even if she'd wanted to. She wished she'd listened to her mother when she'd suggested Maria carry one of those personal alarm things. Past episodes of the programme *Crimewatch* entered her head.

All of a sudden, Maria collided with something, or someone.

"I'm so sorry!" she gasped.

"Don't be sorry." It was the voice of an elderly gentleman. "It's not everyday an attractive young woman bumps into me."

"How do you know what I look like - you can't see me!" gasped Maria.

"I can tell by your voice, my dear. Are you all right - you seem frightened?"

"I'm terrified," replied Maria. "I think someone's following me, and I'm not sure where I am."

"Take my arm - I'm sorry, I don't know your name."

"Maria," she replied shakily.

"Well, Maria, take my arm, and I'll walk you home." She did as she was told. "I'm Bob, by the way," he reassured her.

"Hello, Bob," Maria trembled, feeling weak with relief. She glanced behind her, and listened: whoever she thought had been there had gone, frightened away by the appearance of Bob, she guessed. Or had she imagined it? Sometimes she thought, 'I am my own worst enemy.'

"How can you tell where you're going?" she asked Bob. "I feel completely disorientated."

"I've lived in this village all my life," he replied. "I know every paving stone, hedge, fence, railings and building. My stick helps, of course. Where do you live, Maria?"

"Yew Tree Cottage," she replied.

"I heard someone had moved in there," said Bob. "So what brought you here?"

"I'm the new teacher at the school," replied Maria.

"Of course, I should have guessed. Well, here we are – Yew Tree Cottage."

"Thank you so much," said Maria. "You are my knight in shining armour."

"No problem," replied Bob. "See you around. Well actually, I won't, I'm blind, but you know what I mean."

Maria watched as Bob was enveloped by the fog, his white stick tapping the pavement. She turned her key in the lock, and walked into Yew Tree Cottage, feeling very grateful – and very humbled.

# LIFE BEGINS AT FIFTY

IT WAS AN EARLY MORNING in February; the days were gradually getting longer. The sun shone - a rare occurrence since the previous Autumn. Julie donned her coat, hat, gloves and wellies, and stepped outside. Shadow the dog was ecstatic: the thought of a walk always made him giddy with excitement and anticipation; he trotted eagerly a few steps ahead of her. She was pleased to see the snowdrops in bloom, and daffodil shoots poking their heads out of the earth to reach the light. Julie wanted Spring to arrive now - she was always impatient for warmer weather, but the signs were there.

She walked along a country lane - apart from Shadow, she was alone. This surprised, but pleased her - she didn't feel like talking. She stood to admire the view; Shadow had gone on ahead. How beautiful the countryside looked in the early morning sunlight! The surrounding mountains beckoned her. In the distance was a mountain capped with snow. It reminded her of a Christmas cake her mother had made many years before, when Julie was a child. She remembered how talented her mother had been - she could turn her hand to anything. Sadness enveloped Julie as she thought of her - how cruel life was! Julie's mother had developed Alzheimer's, and had changed into a different person before her death, five years before. She wished euthanasia was legal - her mother wouldn't have wanted to die in the way she did. But, of course, euthanasia wouldn't apply in dementia cases – the powers-that-be would argue that having dementia might deem the patient incapable of making the right decision. There wasn't a day passed by when her mother didn't enter her thoughts - they had been close.

Suddenly she saw movement: a fox crept warily across the meadow. He hadn't seen her, and she hoped Shadow hadn't seen the fox. The fox seemed oblivious of her presence - how handsome he looked! What a shame he caused the farmers such anxiety at lambing time! She wanted to give him a name, but to do so would rob him of his dignity. A sudden bird call startled him, and he ran off. 'What agility!' thought Julie.

As she walked, Julie was lost in thought. Apart from her mother's illness, she had been fortunate. She was married to a man she loved, and had two beautiful children. Her son had married two years before, and she got on well with her daughter-in-law. Last December they had presented Julie with her very first grandchild – a boy. He was beautiful, and doing extremely well – now almost double his birth weight. Her daughter had married last year, and was living nearby, in a bungalow her son-in-law had built. She was so lucky both couples lived locally.

Julie thought that apart from when her children were very young, this was the happiest time of her life. She was now free to do what she wanted. Three years before, she had published a poem book, which had sold very well, and the following summer, she had recorded a CD of poems. The proceeds of both these ventures went to charity - something she was very proud of. She was now working on her second book, which would be published in the summer.

Shadow bounded back to her, wanting to confirm her existence. 'Soon it will be May,' thought Julie.

May was her favourite month: the countryside would take on a greenery beyond expectation, beautifully coloured flowers would decorate the hedgerows, and the sky would be a permanent shade of blue. She always wanted the world to stop in May, and remain there for ever. But of course, Summer would arrive, with its heat, flies and wasps. She had an aversion to all things that buzzed: they were always hell-bent on causing her pain and distress.

Julie glanced at her watch.

"Come along, Shadow," she called. "Breakfast."

Shadow bounded back to her, eager to obey his owner's bidding. Besides, he knew there would be something to eat when they returned to the warm kitchen he knew as home.

# LONELY HEARTS

PAM ARRIVED at the Lemon Tree Café twenty minutes early. Everything had gone well. Her daughter Emily had gone to bed happily, and her baby-sitter had arrived on time. She was meeting Tom, who'd contacted her after she had answered his Lonely Hearts advert in the local newspaper. She sat at a table for two near the window. From her vantage point, she would hopefully see Tom before he saw her. She ordered coffee to help pass the time. She knew Tom was tall, had dark curly hair, and would be smartly dressed. Well, that was what he'd told her.

Pam sat nervously looking around her. She wondered if Tom would be the man of her dreams. The café was quite busy, and as she looked, she thought how unremarkable most faces were, and whatever assumptions she made about her fellow diners, they would probably be as wrong as their assumptions about her. She realised she would not recognise these people in a different setting. Ultimately, the various arrangements of eyes, nose, ears and mouth had more in common than they had apart, and it was only adornment and expression that gave them individuality. Change those, she thought, and anonymity was guaranteed.

She looked through the window - he was late. She watched people scurrying by, faces hidden by umbrellas of varying colours, which were intended to protect them from the persistent drizzle descending from the evening sky. She looked at her watch - it was seven twenty-five. All of a sudden, the door burst open, and

Tom entered the café. She knew him instantly. He looked around, spotted her, and walked purposefully over to her table.

"Pam?" he asked. She nodded. "Sorry I'm late," he announced, breathlessly. "I've been sitting in the Lemon Grove café, two streets away."

"An easy mistake," she answered. "I've only just arrived myself."

"I'll get us a coffee," he said, and walked towards the counter. Pam surreptitiously put her cold coffee cup on the empty table behind her.

When he came back he was smiling - she immediately felt at ease. As he began telling her about himself, she felt she had always known him. He was a reporter for the local newspaper, and made it sound very exciting. When he asked her what she did for a living, she answered, "I'm a Junior School teacher at Grove School."

"I have a niece at that school," he replied.

"What a coincidence!" Pam asked her name.

"Natasha," he answered. Pam knew her well: she was a pretty little girl, her hair plaited into two blond pigtails, who wore dresses with flowers on, and always, red shoes.

"How about a meal?" he suggested. "I know a wonderful little pub just around the corner – I'm starving." Pam agreed. She suddenly realised how hungry she was - she hadn't eaten since lunchtime. Outside in the street, Tom reached for her hand – she reciprocated. It was still raining, but it didn't seem to matter any more. As they entered the pub, the warm air seemed to promise an evening of hospitality. Pam wondered whether this could be the start of something good – only time would tell.

***

# MELANIE AND THE DOG

MELANIE HAD LIVED at Foxen Manor for ten years. Her flat was on the second floor - number twelve to be exact. The Manor consisted of twenty-four flats. She was acquainted with all the people living there: they were a pleasant group - some, very good friends.

Melanie knew her eye-sight was deteriorating, and she was terrified of going blind. Her fears had been confirmed during a visit to her optician.

"You are losing your sight," the optician announced, in a matter-of-fact sort of way. "I suggest you make enquiries with a view to acquiring a guide dog." Melanie left the optician's in a state of shock. She knew Brian, her landlord, was dead against having animals at Foxen Manor, so what on earth was she going to do?

Melanie always turned to her faith at times like these. She believed things happened for a reason, and if she was to go blind, there would be a good reason for it, although at that moment, she had no idea what the reason was.

That afternoon, she made enquiries about getting a guide dog. This proved to be quite easy, as her optician had already been in touch, stating her case was an exceptional one and, in his opinion, she should be allowed a dog immediately. Now, all she had to do was tackle Brian. He was to collect her rent at seven that evening; she rehearsed their forthcoming conversation in her head.

At seven on the dot, there was a knock at her door: Brian was a stickler for punctuality. He entered with his usual brusque manner. She decided to come straight to the point:

"Brian," she announced, "I'm losing my sight, and my optician has recommended I get a guide dog - in fact, the dog's arriving tomorrow." Brian was at a loss for words – quite taken aback for a change. Suddenly, he regained his poise, and said, "Melanie, you know the rules – no animals. If I make an exception with you, who knows where it will end? There could be cats and hamsters all over the Manor. No, I will not allow it." Melanie was expecting this.

"Brian, I am getting a guide dog, and if you won't allow him on the premises, I will vacate my flat." Brian looked shocked, but said, "As you wish," and left without another word.

Melanie calmly knocked on her neighbour Mary's door, and explained her predicament. Melanie's problem spread like wildfire through Foxen Manor. All her neighbours were outraged at Brian's reaction.

Brian's mind was in turmoil as he left Melanie's flat. He liked her - well, more than liked her, so why was he hell-bent on ruining any relationship they might have? He didn't want her to leave the Manor any more than she did. He was his own worst enemy sometimes. He slept fitfully that night.

The following evening, Brian arrived home from work to find all the occupants of Foxen Manor standing outside, waiting for him. They were fronted by Melanie, and standing next to her was the most adorable Labrador he had ever seen. Nevertheless, he marched up to the group and asked, "What's going on?" Melanie replied. "My neighbours have heard about my dilemma, and decided that unless you agree to my having a guide dog, they will follow my example, and leave Foxen Manor."

Brian knew when he was beaten. "In that case, against my better judgement, I will allow you your dog, but yours is an exceptional circumstance - the 'No Pets' rule still stands." There was a loud cheer from the gathering as they filtered back into their individual apartments. Melanie and Brian exchanged a smile.

"Thank you, Brian," she said, relieved that all had gone well.

"He's a very handsome dog," announced Brian. "I trust he'll be well-behaved."

"Of course," replied Melanie. "I'll make sure of it." Brian nodded, and headed back to his own apartment. She stood there watching him. 'The power of the throng, very good friends, and an endearing Labrador,' thought Melanie.

# PERFECT DAY

SARAH AWOKE TO THE SOUND of rain tapping at her bedroom window. She jumped out of bed, and opened the curtains - her heart plummeted. The sky was grey, apart from a small patch of blue. A neighbour's comment from childhood suddenly came into her mind: 'There's enough blue to make a sailor a pair of pants.' 'Well,' thought Sarah, 'there's enough blue to make a sailor two pairs of pants.' She had prayed for weeks for a dry day, and felt rather annoyed her prayers hadn't been answered. Looking towards the ceiling she exclaimed, "I don't ask for much – you could have granted me this one wish!"

She reached for her dressing gown, and went downstairs to make a cup of tea. She put one teabag in the teapot; then, hearing movement from her daughter's bedroom, she decided she had better put in two. Her daughter was getting married today, and what better than a cup of tea to start the day.

"It's raining, Mum," said Emma, as she flounced into the kitchen.

"Tell me something I don't know," replied Sarah. They both sat at the table, deep in thought. Sarah switched on the television, just in time to see the weather forecast. "Look," she said, "there's a yellow sun on us this afternoon – we might be lucky." Emma didn't look impressed. Suddenly, she changed her attitude:

"Well, we can't do anything about it, so I'm not going to let it spoil my special day," she announced.

All too soon, the hairdresser and beautician turned up – the house was a flurry of activity. Emma's hair was coaxed, with the help of tongs, into barrel curls, and looked amazing when her tiara and veil were in place. Her make-up looked perfect – not too much, but enough to accentuate her eyes, lips and cheekbones. Sarah shed a tear, and couldn't speak for a moment, when she saw her daughter looking so beautiful in her wedding dress.

"Please don't cry, Mum," pleaded Emma. "You'll start me off."

"Your dad will be so proud," said Sarah. At that moment Steve, Emma's dad, walked in, and stood there motionless.

"Well, say something, Dad!" exclaimed Emma. Steve smiled slowly:

"Ready?" he asked. Steve was never very good at compliments, or showing his emotions, but Emma could see he was visibly moved.

When it was time to leave for the church, Emma took her dad's arm, and looked up at him. She looked so much like Sarah that Steve was taken back to his own wedding day thirty years before - it felt like yesterday. It had rained that day too, when they'd entered the church, but there was bright sunshine when they'd emerged. What he remembered most was a huge rainbow, which the photographer had taken advantage of very quickly, before it disappeared - the resulting photos had been stunning.

As the wedding car drove towards the church, neighbours came out of their houses to watch and wave. Emma had never felt so important. The rain had stopped, and the sun was out.

"Perhaps we're going to be lucky after all, Dad," she said, excitedly.

"I think so, Emma," he replied. "Look!" They had reached the church, and arcing over the church, was the biggest rainbow Emma had ever seen. She gasped:

"It's an omen – it's going to be a perfect day."

# PRINCE

S HE WAS BROUGHT UP on a smallholding, consisting
of three acres of land, in the Welsh countryside.
Her best friend, during her childhood years, was a
sheepdog collie called Prince. Prince was her constant
companion, and as she was an only child, he was a
very important part of her life.

Her parents were keen gardeners, who grew all their
own vegetables and fruit. They also had five beehives
so, as a result, they produced their own honey – it was
a very healthy upbringing.

She remembered owning a plastic, orange-coloured
mouth organ, and when she blew into it, Prince would
howl. She never discovered whether it was a howl of
joy, or despair – she hoped it was joy. They often played
with a short length of flexible rubber-tubing – they
spent many happy hours running up and down the
field, she at one end of the tubing, and Prince at the
other. The one thing Prince was afraid of was thunder:
he would follow her up the garden, and even into the
house, both places usually completely out of bounds
for him. He didn't like bumblebees either – he would
snap, and usually injure them. She would come to their
rescue by building a makeshift refuge to protect them.
They usually died, but she did all she could.

One day, she heard a bloodcurdling howl – Prince
had tried to jump over a barbed-wire fence, but his fur
caught on the spikes, so he was balancing precariously
on the top. She immediately ran to his aid, and lifted
him gently to the ground – this action, of course,
increased the bond between them.

As the years passed, Prince became deaf. The day she went to stay with relatives, Prince disappeared. She hadn't wanted to go, but couldn't disappoint her cousins. She rang home every evening to ask if Prince had returned – the answer each time was, 'No.' He'd been missing for a day or two before, but never a whole week.

Following her return, she and her dad went in search of him. They drove around, and asked various different people, but no one had seen him. Having been unsuccessful, they drove home along a main road, when she noticed an unusual black bundle on the grass verge. Her dad stopped the car, and went to investigate. She couldn't believe it was Prince - didn't want to - but she knew it was him. The tears flowed then. She'd known in her heart something awful had happened – until then, she'd had hope. Obviously Prince had wandered down to the main road, about a mile from their home, and simply hadn't heard the car that killed him. She felt anger at the driver – 'Why couldn't people drive more carefully? Did they not realise Prince belonged to a family who loved him?'

She was glad they'd found him – at least now they knew where he was, and what had happened. Her dad, and a colleague from work, buried Prince where he lay.

Each time she drove by that spot in later years she would remember him. She had loved him so much, and knew he'd loved her too. She wished she'd been present at the end, to ease his passing. – she couldn't bear the thought he'd died alone, and in pain. She hoped it had been instantaneous. They had shared so much – he had made her childhood a happy one. She would never forget her faithful childhood companion.

# THE MISSING BUTTON

VIOLET WAS A LOVELY, little old lady, aged ninety-two. She lived in a village in the centre of the English countryside, and every Thursday at 10 a.m. went to collect her pension from the Post Office. She got up early on Thursdays so she could reach the Post Office in good time - she hated being late. She supposed this habit stemmed from her time as secretary at the Bank. Her job was to make sure her boss' life ran smoothly, and this she achieved with cheerful determination, and competence.

Violet, after collecting her pension, always made sure she put it in her handbag before leaving the Post Office. She would then walk back to her cottage on the other side of the village. She was a creature of habit, so her routine never varied.

However, one particular Thursday, whilst walking back to her cottage, Violet was unaware she was being followed. Suddenly, she heard someone run up behind her, snatch her bag, and run off. Despite her increasing years, Violet was not without strength. She made a grab at the person, and a coat button came off in her hand. Badly shaken, she sat by the road side. Her legs felt like jelly - she felt violated. She opened her hand to reveal the button: it was unusual – black, and shaped like a horse's head. By this time, a young couple she knew as Tim and Leah had arrived to check she was ok. Violet assured them she was fine, and showed them the button. Leah gasped:

"I gave a coat, with buttons like that, to the charity shop yesterday! I'll pop back now, and ask if they can remember who bought it." Off she went, while Tim walked Violet to her cottage. Very soon, Leah was back.

"It was bought by a teenager, who's just moved into the village with her mother. Apparently, her mother is unwell - a terminal illness."

Suddenly, there was knock at the door. Violet opened it to find a teenager standing there.

"I'm so sorry," she said. "My name's Carol - I took your bag. Did I hurt you?"

"No, you didn't," replied Violet. "I was just a bit shaken."

Carol handed the bag to Violet.

"It's all intact: check it if you like."

"I'm sure there's no need," replied Violet. "Please come in." Carol hesitated when she saw Tim and Leah, but entered, shyly.

"I think I have something of yours," said Violet, handing Carol the button.

"Thank you," replied Carol. "I knew I'd lost it when I took your bag."

"I hear your mum's unwell," said Violet.

"Yes," replied Carol, "but she is hoping the chemotherapy will give her a few more years - we'll have to wait and see."

"I'm sorry," said Violet. "It must be very difficult. Is your dad around?"

"My dad died soon after I was born," replied Carol. "There's only Mum and I now. We lived on an estate in Liverpool before we came here – Mum wanted to live in the country."

"Have you made any friends of your own age yet?" asked Leah.

"Sort of, but I've only been at my new school for two

weeks - I suppose these things take time. I have lots of friends in Liverpool: I miss them so much."

"You'll have to give your new school time to get used to you," said Tim. "I've only just met you, and I think you're very brave. It's not easy to return something you've stolen, and apologise. I know you shouldn't have taken it in the first place, but you know that, and I don't think you'll do it again."

"No, I won't," replied Carol. "I don't know why I did it. I suppose it's been a big change moving here, but that's no excuse. I'm so sorry."

"Let's forget about it, and have a nice cup of tea," said Violet. "Tea always makes things seem better, don't you think? And if you ever need anyone to talk to, Carol, come and knock at my door - I'm usually always here."

# FRUSTRATION

S HE PUT HER PHONE DOWN slowly, her mind in turmoil - he was back on the whisky! He'd denied it, of course, but she knew. She always knew. The most obvious clue was he talked slowly, with long pauses, as if he were dredging up some snippet of knowledge from the depths of his brain. He'd been doing so well - she could only imagine what had gone wrong this time. She knew he was an alcoholic, but had tried so hard to understand and help him in so many ways.

The main emotion she felt was disappointment - he'd let her down. But more importantly, he'd let himself down. Disappointment coursed through her veins, followed very quickly by frustration. What could she do? Nothing at this moment in time, she guessed. He would have to sober up first. Trying to reason with him when he'd had a drink was a complete waste of time, and he simply wouldn't remember the conversation anyway. When he rang her, having had a drink, he always refused to listen to what she had to say, and was constantly interrupting. It was hopeless.

She'd suspected there was a problem – his texts that day were odd, to say the least, and slightly mis-spelt. But she'd brushed her dark thoughts aside, giving him the benefit of the doubt. Having her suspicions confirmed was not pleasant. In fact, it made her angry. How dare he be so selfish! He didn't give a thought to those around him who were directly affected by his drinking. He had responsibilities, but how could he fulfil them in his drunken state? It would have a knock-on effect on everyone.

She wondered whether he realised the effect his drinking had on her. She was beginning to dread answering the phone, or getting a text. Was this the 'cyber-bullying' they talked about, she wondered? Whatever it was, she was getting very tired of the abuse he threw at her - he could be so nasty.

She guessed his drinking was probably a result of not having confronted some deep-seated issue from the past - from childhood perhaps. So that when another, however minor problem came along, he felt unable to cope, and reached for the bottle. She knew alcoholism was an illness, and that alcoholics were usually lonely, depressed people. If only they could see that when they drank, people stayed away, exacerbating their loneliness and depression. Perhaps she would never fully understand why her friend had this compulsion to drink, but she'd tried so hard.

Whatever the problem was this time, why hadn't he rung her first, before turning to the bottle? He'd promised he would. And if not her, then the Drinks Counsellor was on hand - although, only during Office Hours, she guessed. When he drank, he became someone she didn't know. No, that wasn't entirely true: she was beginning to know this *alter ego* very well - too well.

The truth was, he was two people — the loving, thoughtful, caring person, who was happy to help and do anything for anyone. And then, there was the unpleasant, argumentative, demanding, sometimes violent person, whom nobody liked. He was intelligent, so why couldn't he see what he was doing? So many people had life-threatening conditions they could do nothing about, but he was playing Russian roulette with his life. She'd lost count of the number of times she'd raced to the hospital because he'd been rushed in, having received an injury, due to his drinking.

When he drank, he would say and do things he would never say and do normally. She couldn't understand why he wasn't embarrassed by the way he behaved. She thought she would have been mortified, were the boot on the other foot.

Alcohol was to blame for most of his problems. Maybe one day he would wake up and realise that. She hoped so. Until then, she would try and be there for him, and simply take a step back when he drank. She refused to be the object of his anger any more – his emotional punchbag. Hopefully, one day, with the right help, he would be able to give up the alcohol altogether, and she prayed that that would happen before she was forced to walk away for good.

# THE MISSING MEDAL

MAUDE, a spritely eighty-year-old, lived alone since losing her husband John five years before, after his long battle with cancer. She still missed him desperately, but tried to keep busy with her many hobbies, one of which was gardening, although it wasn't getting any easier as the years passed. There would come a time when she would need help, especially with the weeding.

John had been in the Army, and one of Maude's most treasured possessions was a small box containing medals with which John had been decorated, after the Second World War. Her favourite was a silver one, for an act of bravery. The medals were kept in a sideboard, behind a pile of Agatha Christie books.

Maude was eligible for *'Meals on Wheels'*, so every day at twelve-thirty, her dinner would arrive in a foil container. This she looked forward to, and not having to cook it herself was an added bonus. Most days, her meals were delivered by Pauline, a chatty young lady of about thirty, but on Tuesdays, Peter would deliver. Peter had also been in the Army, so he and Maude had something in common. As hers was the last house on Peter's route, he would often stop and chat, and had been shown John's medals many times.

One Tuesday evening, after watching the News, Maude decided to look at John's medals again, only to find the silver one missing. She tipped the contents of the box onto the table, and went through them meticulously. No - it definitely wasn't there. Maude began to panic. It had certainly been there the last time she'd looked.

Suddenly, her eye caught sight of something shiny on the floor by the sideboard. She picked it up, and realised it was a button. The button was unusual, because it was a metal one - with a slightly raised soldier's head on the front. She knew immediately where she'd seen that button before - it was on Peter's jacket - his navy one. Had Peter taken the medal? She couldn't believe it of him. She went to bed that night, feeling very uneasy. What was she going to do? She slept, eventually, only to be woken by disturbing dreams.

The following morning she checked the box again: perhaps she'd been mistaken - but the medal wasn't there. Suddenly, Maude heard her back door open, and her grandson Michael walked in. He often called on his way to school to check she was well.

"Hi, Gran," he said. "I'm just returning Granddad's medal. Thank you so much for letting me borrow it." Maude was astounded.

"You mean you've got the medal?" she asked, feeling relief flooding through her.

"Of course, Gran. Remember, you lent it to me last Friday - for my school project." Maude thought, but couldn't recall. "You were on the telephone with the Gas Company – they'd overcharged you," Michael explained. All of a sudden she remembered: she had been on the phone when Michael called, and must have given her consent, but it had completely slipped her mind – she had been so annoyed with the Gas Company.

"Come and give your Gran a big hug," she said.

"Gran, I'll be late for school," moaned Michael, but he didn't really mind – he was very fond of his Gran.

After Michael left, Maud scolded herself:

"You shouldn't jump to conclusions – there's always a perfectly reasonable explanation," she told herself, feeling very relieved indeed

# THE NEXT WORLD

D AVID OPENED HIS EYES. It was dark; he felt cold, and the ground was uncomfortable. He wondered where he was, and suddenly remembered: earlier that afternoon, he'd been returning from the field, next to his house, when he'd stumbled over something, he knew not what. The next thing he knew, he'd fallen, and was unable to get up. He'd managed, with great difficulty, to crawl slowly, though painfully, into his yard, but was unable, for some reason, to climb the two concrete steps, which would lead him to the sanctity of his kitchen, via the back door. Perhaps exhaustion was to blame – he certainly felt tired. He couldn't remember what time he fell, but it had been daylight. Eventually, he'd crawled to the wall of his garden – at least here, there was a little shelter.

He must have dozed. He had no concept of time, but, as it was dark, he guessed it could be any time between 5 p.m. and 7 a.m. It was early March, and the nights were still long. It was a blessing it wasn't raining, or, even worse, snowing, and, compared to the two previous nights, was reasonably mild. He wondered whether he could survive the night outside – he was, after all, 89 years old.

A sudden sound interrupted his reverie – he looked up, and saw what looked like an enormous gaggle of geese, or ducks, flying overhead – thousands of them. He had never seen so many birds at once, and they were making the most appalling racket. He wondered where they were heading.

David must have slept again, because when he woke, he saw a beautiful garden full of pink flowers - millions of them. He'd never seen so many flowers before. There were several beautiful women picking the flowers and, when asked what they were doing, they replied they needed the flowers to make wine.

David thought he was going mad – was this a hallucination, or, was he close to death, and getting a glimpse of Heaven? He suspected the latter. He knew of other people who had had a similar experience.

His next recollection was hearing his daughter's voice: she told him he was in hospital.

Remarkably, he survived. He had been outside, on the ground, for twenty-four hours. He had pneumonia, and gangrene, but was expected to make a full recovery. The doctors told him he was lucky to be alive.

Six weeks later he was allowed home. He felt emotional – he had been through a very traumatic experience. But he was no longer afraid of dying. When his time came, he would go happily. He knew what to expect, and was almost looking forward to it - he couldn't wait to be reunited with his beloved wife.

\*\*\*

# THE ROBIN

SHE WAS WASHING the last remaining breakfast dishes when she saw him. She glanced up to find him looking straight at her. He stood on spindly legs, his red breast in complete contrast with the snowy background. The snow was about six inches deep, and, as there had been a sharp frost during the night, it sparkled in the early morning sunshine. What a beautiful Christmas card this scene would make, she thought. Snow was beautiful as long as it was undisturbed. She stood, transfixed. She did not move, in case he flew away. The breeze ruffled his feathers, which reminded her how cold he must be feeling.

Someone once told her robins represent loved ones in heaven - they come with a message. What a lovely myth, she thought. But was it a myth? Probably. She thought how wonderful it would be to get a message from her mother, who had passed away six years before. She still missed her dreadfully. Not a day went by but that she thought of her. A lady cut off in her prime. Alzheimer's was such a cruel condition, robbing its victims of their dignity, and eventually, their life.

At that moment, the shrill sound of the telephone woke her from her reverie. She moved suddenly, and, of course, the robin flew away. It was her editor, confirming that her second book of poetry would be delivered that day. This was excellent news. She had waited a long time for this call.

She moved back to the window, and was amazed to see the robin was there again, looking as perky as ever. Now she understood - the robin had come with a message. It was a message of congratulations. Her mother had always been the first to praise her when she achieved something. She had missed that since she'd gone. Her mum was still looking out for her - she was convinced of it now. The robin was looking at her, turning his head to one side.

Something distracted her. She glanced away, and when she turned back, he was gone. She felt calm, and contented. Whether the robin had come with a message, or not, didn't matter - she had felt her mother's presence.

# TOM

TOM SAT, SURVEYING THE CLOSE, with his acute feline intelligence. There were quite a few cats out tonight, but that wasn't surprising - it was a warm summer's evening. Nothing untoward was happening, but he'd stay on watch for a little while longer anyway.

He'd been here three months, and had learnt quite a lot in that time. In fact, when Tom arrived, he was taken in as a stray. His now owners, an elderly couple – John and Madge, took to him immediately. He was well fed, loved, and wanted for nothing.

But, in actual fact, Tom wasn't a cat at all - he was an alien, who had come down to earth in the guise of a cat, so that he would be accepted. No one suspected. His mission was to learn as much as he could about what went on here - a planet his species knew very little about.

He didn't think anyone saw him arrive – well, he hoped not, anyway. He was dropped off by his spaceship on a piece of waste ground. There was no one around, and if there was, who would believe them?

He'd chosen to make his home in this particular Close because of the number of cats already there. His intention was to fit in as easily and as quickly as possible. He'd settled in very well, although the other cats were slightly in awe of him. They knew he was different is some way, but couldn't quite put their paw on it. They thought him to be superior, and looked as though he were in charge, which suited Tom very well - they respected him.

The following morning he was back at his post. He saw the milkman arrive – Tom had discovered he liked milk, especially when his owners warmed it up for him. The postman came and went – this fascinated Tom – the postman would post pieces of paper through a gap in the door! Very strange indeed. He watched the children walk to somewhere they called 'School'. They always had a kind word for him, and often stroked him too. He'd worked out that if he purred, they stayed that little bit longer. They all wore the same clothes when going to school – he guessed they didn't have a choice. The ladies in the Close went out, usually in the mornings, carrying bags, and came home later with something in them – food usually. Well, that's what his owners brought home anyway, much to Tom's delight.

Tom knew he was due to go home that day – he could sense it. He wasn't sure he wanted to go though – he liked it here. He'd also become very friendly with a black and white female cat, who lived nearby. Her name was Tilly - she was lovely, and spent quite a lot of time with him. But go he must.

After his tea that evening, he sat by the door, waiting to be let out. Madge came and opened the door and, out of the ordinary said,

"Goodbye, Tom."

Tom turned and looked at her – how did she know? She'd never said goodbye when letting him out before. He walked down the path, and turned again. Both John and Madge were on the doorstep – Madge dabbing her eyes with a handkerchief. They did know!

Tom walked the short distance to the piece of waste ground, where his spaceship had left him. Of course, Tilly came too. He looked up, and in the far distance, he could see a light. The light gradually got bigger, and sure enough, his spaceship arrived. Something made him turn around – John and Madge were standing on the edge of the waste ground. They both waved goodbye. Tilly sat at their feet. Tears filled Tom's eyes.

'What's wrong with me?' he thought – 'aliens don't cry. Obviously some of their human traits have rubbed off on me – how strange.'

He walked up the steps to the spaceship, and looked back again – they were still there. Tom raised a paw in salute. John and Madge waved back. Then he was gone.

'I will come back soon,' thought Tom. 'There is so much more to learn, and they were so kind to me. And maybe, Tilly will have kittens. Now that would be interesting - and certainly, a valid reason to return.'

# THE NEW FRIEND

ELAINE SAT ON THE PARK BENCH, deep in thought. Today was her birthday – she was ten. Her mind was in turmoil - her parents had just told her, she was adopted. She'd taken the news calmly - perhaps it was shock. She hadn't asked any questions - she couldn't think of any. Her parents reassured her, and told her she was special – that's why they'd chosen her.

Elaine had walked out of the house, and crossed the road to the park – she always came here to think. Her parents were quite happy with this: they knew she was quite safe, because they could see the bench clearly from their sitting room window.

Lots of questions ran around in Elaine's head now, but she needed to think about them before she approached her parents. She didn't want to hurt them, she loved them, and her childhood up to now, had been brilliant.

She suddenly became aware of an elderly lady sitting on the same bench, watching her.

"Hello," said the lady. "My name's Margaret. You seem troubled - can I help?"

"I don't know," replied Elaine. "My thoughts are all mixed up at the moment."

"Well, a trouble shared is a trouble halved," said Margaret. Elaine thought Margaret looked very old, but then anyone over the age of fifty seemed old to Elaine.

"It's my birthday – I'm ten," said Elaine.

"Happy Birthday," said Margaret. "And - you're upset - because?"

"My mum and dad have just told me I'm adopted," replied Elaine.

"I see," said Margaret. "We have something in common then – I was adopted too."

Elaine was astounded. "But how did you feel when you found out?" She asked.

"Much the same as you do now, I expect," replied Margaret. "It was a long time ago, but I remember it as though it were yesterday."

"What did you do?" asked Elaine.

"Nothing - at the time," replied Margaret. "I knew my parents loved me very much, and I loved them. Then, when I was eighteen, I met my birth mother."

Elaine couldn't believe what she was hearing. "Didn't your mum and dad mind?" she asked.

"No, not at all," replied Margaret. "I talked to them about it, and they were happy for me to go ahead. It took a while to find her, but eventually I did. Remember, when you're an adult, you can do what you like, within reason. As long as you don't hurt anybody."

Elaine was quiet for a few minutes – she needed to digest this new information. An ice-cream van's jingle shattered the silence. Normally, Elaine would have asked her parents for money for an ice cream, but today, her mind was occupied with more pressing matters.

"So when I grow up, I can find my birth-mother?"

"Yes, if you want to," answered Margaret. "But talk to your parents first – they may be able to tell you who she is, and why she didn't feel she could look after you."

Elaine absorbed this information. Eventually she said, "But perhaps I won't want to find out."

"Perhaps you won't," said Margaret. "You won't be grown up for a few years, so you can take your time, and make up your mind when the time comes."

"Do you still see your birth-mother now?" asked Elaine.

"No," replied Margaret – both my mothers are dead, but I consider myself to be very fortunate – I had two lovely mothers, whereas most people only have one."

Elaine made a decision - "It's my birthday party this afternoon," she said. "Will you come?"

"I'm not sure your mother would want me there," replied Margaret.

"Of course she will," said Elaine. "Look!"

Margaret turned around to see Elaine's mum waving at them from her sitting room window, a few yards from the park. Both Margaret and Elaine waved back. Elaine said, "All my friends are coming, so you'd be very welcome."

"In that case," replied Margaret, "I'd be very happy to come."

They both walked towards Elaine's house, where her mother was waiting to greet them.

***

# BONO

I WAS ADOPTED when I was eleven weeks old. Dad came to see my brothers and sisters and me, and I lay down on his foot. He chose me to take home, but he says I chose him, which I suppose I did, in a way.

I'm a handsome Jack Russell. Well, I think so anyway. And, I'm unique! One of my ears always sticks up, which makes me different, and that's an advantage, surely?

I live in a bungalow, and it's great – lots of space to run around. I'm interested in everything, and always know what's going on. I've learnt to know exactly what Mum and Dad are saying, especially, *'Dentastick'* and 'Supper!'

Actually, I have two homes, because Mum and Dad go out to work. While they're away, I stay at the farm next door with Nain and Taid. They have a Kelpie/Collie-Cross bitch called Pip. Pip is twelve years old, and will play with me - but only when she feels like it. And, if I get amorous, she gets a bit cross, and snarls at me. I suppose she can't be bothered with that kind of thing any more: she doesn't seem to realise - I'm a red-blooded male!

What I like best about the farm is the Quad-Bike – Taid has attached a green plastic box in front of the handle-bars, in which I sit. I love it – I get to see where we're going before anyone else. Pip stands/sits behind Taid on the seat – it's actually quite a clever balancing act. I think she leans on Taid for support though. I love the tractor too. I get in the cab with Taid, or whoever's driving - I'm not fussy.

They're building a barn-conversion at the farm, and sometimes the builders play with me. There's a big ball which I love, but one of the builders has put it high up, out of reach, so I sit staring at it, hoping someone will take pity on me, and retrieve it.

One of the disadvantages of playing on the farm is, I get very muddy. As a result, Taid washes and dries my feet before I'm allowed in the house. I hate this. I growl to voice my disapproval. I wouldn't bite, but I give the impression I might.

Once I'm in, I fetch my little ball and push it along with my blue, plastic bone. It acts like a mini snow-plough. If Nain's not busy, she'll throw the ball for me, and I'll bring it back. I can spend hours doing this, but Nain always tires before I do. Eventually, I jump on the sofa and sleep on my special blanket. I dream of all the rabbits I've chased that day.

By evening, I'm restless, because I know Mum or Dad will fetch me soon. I wonder whether I'll have a shower with Mum tonight – she often insists, after a day on the farm! If Dad comes to speak to Mum when we're in the shower, I stand in between them and growl. I don't allow Dad near Mum when I think she's in a vulnerable situation. They laugh at me though, but I don't think it's funny at all. I'm just doing my job – protecting Mum.

I hear a sound! I jump onto the arm of the chair by the window. I balance, with my two front paws on the window-sill, one back paw on the arm, and the other in the air. I get a really good view of the yard from here. I peer into the darkness, and yes, I see a light. Is it Dad's white van, or Mum's car? It's a car! It's Mum! I run into the kitchen, and jump up and down (I can jump really high, as high as the door-handle!) until Nain opens the door. I race down the hall, and wait impatiently until Mum comes in. I jump into her arms: it's good to feel her warmth, and smell her perfume.

Occasionally, Mum takes me to the Vet because I get itchy paws. The last time I went, we entered the waiting- room, only to find a large black cat sitting in a cat-basket on her owner's knee. The feline took one look at me, and emitted a throaty growl. I barked, but then hid behind Mum – the cat was significantly larger than I.

Eventually, it was my turn to see the Vet. Mum lifted me onto a table, and the Vet pushed something up my bottom! Then, he took it out again, and said, "Well, his temperature's ok."

It's all very undignified! And, I had an injection - it hurt! I was given two different types of tablet. I remember thinking, 'There's no way I'm taking them!'

When we arrived home, Mum said, "Now - be a good boy, and take your medication." I didn't react. Mum took a piece of sausage out of the fridge, and pushed one of the tablets into it, and gave it to me. I ate the sausage, and spat out the tablet. Mum frowned; she then pushed the tablet into some cheese. I love cheese. Again, I ate the cheese, and spat out the tablet. Mum said, "Right!" She picked me up, and said, "Open your mouth." When I wouldn't, she said, "Bono!" I opened my mouth, and she popped the tablet in. She then massaged my throat, and the tablet disappeared. It wasn't so bad really. I suppose I shouldn't be naughty, because I love my mum, and I know she only does these things because she loves me too.

Just then, Dad came home. I know his routine: he'll make himself a cup of tea, pick up a packet of biscuits - ginger crunch creams - and sit in front of the television. I sidle up to him on the sofa. If he's in a good mood, he'll give me a piece of biscuit - maybe more than one. I can't help drooling – they look so good. He gives me two pieces - I know that's my limit.

I wonder if Dad's going out tonight. I sort of hope he is, because then, I will get to sleep on the bed, with Mum. I think it's a secret, so I won't tell Dad, if Mum doesn't.

So, you see, the sole reason I was put on this earth, was to protect Mum. I think I make a very good job of it too: Mum's always safe - when I'm around.

**BONO**

# PIP

MY DAUGHTER AND I walked from the barn, tears streaming down our faces. We had just said our final goodbyes to our Kelpie/Collie-Cross, Pip. It was dark, and it was raining – why was the weather always at its worst, when sad things happened? Pip had looked so comfortable in her warm bed of straw. She had no inkling that the next day she was going to the Vet's, and wasn't expected to return.

When the Vet called at the farm a few days previously, on another matter, he'd examined Pip, who had some unsightly lumps on her underside. He'd said Pip would need an x-ray, and if it showed she had internal tumours as well (which he thought she probably had), then it would be kinder to put her to sleep.

The following morning, my husband took Pip to the Vet's. He was putting on a brave face, but I knew how he must be feeling – Pip was his shadow.

Mid-morning, my daughter rang to say she'd had a text message from her friend, who worked at the Vet's, to say Pip was undergoing an operation (a mammary strip) to remove the outer tumours – her chest x-ray was clear. This news was so unexpected, tears sprang into my eyes again. But this time, they were happy tears. This turnaround in events made me feel euphoric. I called the Vet's mid-afternoon, and was told Pip was out in the garden, and recovering well. I couldn't believe it: I'd been so convinced I wouldn't see her again.

Pip came home the following day, complete with cone, to a huge welcome. She had pills to take, of course – painkillers and antibiotics. Despite her ordeal, she was very soon back to her old self – full of enthusiasm.

But four weeks later, something was wrong – Pip was holding her head at a funny angle, and grunting. She was taken back to the Vet's for another x-ray – of her throat, this time. I'd heard nothing all day, and presumed all was well. After all, 'No news is good news,' isn't it?

My husband came home from a meeting late afternoon, and I asked if he'd heard from the Vet's. His face was grave when he said, "Yes, it's bad news. The Vet rang, and said Pip was very poorly – she had a cancerous tumour in her throat, which had burst. They've had to let her go!"

The call had come half-way through the meeting. How he'd managed to concentrate for the remainder of the afternoon, I don't know. He said the meeting was a distraction – perhaps it was.

I was in shock. How on earth could this have happened? Why hadn't they x-rayed her throat the first time around? All kinds of emotions ran through my head – anger, frustration, sadness, and a very deep sense of loss. How could life be so cruel? She had come back to us a healthy dog, we'd thought. To have her taken away from us suddenly like this was so unfair. I thought of my daughter, who'd also been at the meeting: I knew how devastated she would be at the news.

I had a Dance Class to take that evening, and knew the only way I could cope was not to see my daughter beforehand. I was having great difficulty keeping it together as it was. Somehow, I found the strength to take the Class, and hoped no one would notice the turmoil within me.

The following day I saw my daughter, and we wept together. We both felt drained, and exhausted. My husband brought Pip home, and buried her in a place she'd loved to go. "We'll plant some snowdrops there," he said. We will never forget Pip – she was an adorable dog - always placid, and friendly. When she lay down, her paws were often crossed – a trait inherited from her mother, we've been told. My husband looks so lonely without her – she was always at his side. When I go for a walk, she's conspicuous by her absence. My daughter even felt Pip's presence when she took her dog Bono for a walk recently. She even spoke to Pip, so real was the experience.

We will recover from this tragedy one day, but for the moment, we will live life one day at a time.

My three-year-old grandson, on hearing the news, said, "Pippi died. But it's OK, because Taid put her in the ground, and she's having a nice long rest, and she'll become part of the world." I can't improve on that.

PIP

# THE MEETING

ANNABEL LOOKED AT HER WATCH - for the tenth time in as many minutes: he was late. She was meeting her dad Brian, today, for the very first time.

Brian had only been in the Army for two months when Gwen, her mother, received notification that he was missing, presumed dead. Gwen was three months pregnant at the time. Devastated though Gwen was, she had decided to bring her daughter up as well as she could, and provide her with all the information she could find about her father. She never married, and devoted her life to Annabel.

When Annabel was eighteen, she decided to find out more about her father's death, only to find he wasn't dead at all - only badly injured. She was also told that a blow to the head had caused him to lose his memory, which had only recently started to return.

So here she was, sitting on a park bench, waiting for him. When she had spoken to him on the phone, he had suggested the park — neutral ground, she supposed. It was a Friday morning, and reasonably quiet. She watched a man walking his Alsatian dog, or rather, the Alsatian was walking his owner. Annabel wondered why some dogs tugged on their lead like that - it only made them choke. You'd think they'd learn from experience. There was a small child sitting in a pushchair, eating an ice cream, the mother chatting to a friend. Annabel smiled — there was more ice cream in the child's hair and on his face than was getting into his mouth.

"Hello," came a voice. Annabel jumped. She hadn't noticed the man approaching. "Annabel?" he asked.

"Yes," she replied, with a start. Everything she had planned to say deserted her.

"I don't know why I'm asking," Brian said. "You're the image of your mother. I'd have known you anywhere." He sat down beside her. Annabel stared at him.

"I'm sorry," she said, "but you're not like I imagined - you're older."

"But you must have realised - any photos you have of me are from twenty years ago," he replied. Yes, of course, how silly she was - for some reason, she hadn't imagined an older man.

"Where have you been?" she asked.

"Well, I was in hospital, for a long time," he replied. It was then she noticed the stick.

"Can you walk unaided?"

"No, my right leg was broken in several different places: I'm very lucky to be alive."

"Are you married?" asked Annabel.

"No, I'm not. Your mum was the only woman I've ever really loved. Has she married in the meantime?"

"No - she's had one or two men friends, but no one special." They both digested this information – there was hope. "I had all these questions lined up, but now, I can't remember any of them," said Annabel.

"Me too," replied Brian. "Shall we take a walk?"

"But your leg!" exclaimed Annabel.

"Let *me* worry about my leg. As long as we walk slowly, I can cope."

Father and daughter walked together through the park, enjoying each other's company. Annabel couldn't erase the thought that perhaps Brian and her mum would rekindle their relationship, given time. Brian's thoughts were of a similar nature, but for the present, he was content to build a relationship with his daughter.

# THE WEDDING DRESS

WHEN SHE AWOKE that sunny October morning, the first object Katy espied was her beautiful brocade wedding-dress hanging on the wardrobe door. Her mother had sewn it, with so many hours of love going into every stitch. Today, Katy was getting married. She glanced at the clock - it was only 7a.m. The house was silent, so she hurriedly got dressed, and descended the stairs softly. Jim the dog was ecstatic to see anyone around at this hour, especially on a Saturday. Katy let herself out, careful of the latch, and walked down the garden path. Jim was already ahead of her, and waiting patiently at the gate. Katy didn't have to think about where she was going - her feet already knew. She walked down the lane, through a gate, and across a field. She then started to climb a path which wound its way up a mountainside. She had walked this particular path hundreds of times, and each time she would see something new. Today, the spiders' webs, covered in dew, glistened, reflecting the early morning sunshine. There was a chill in the air, but as there were no clouds floating in the clear blue sky, she knew it was going to be a lovely sunny day. Jim was well ahead of her, still agile despite his age. Katy hurried to catch up with him, but Jim had bounded off after a rabbit or hare. He'd be back when he got bored, or whatever he'd been chasing had outrun him.

Very soon she reached the summit, and stood gazing at the panoramic view. Even though she'd been here many times before, the view always took her breath away. The fields looked like a patchwork quilt of brown, green and yellow, and the river meandering through it resembled silver thread. The lake in the distance had the appearance of a grey omelette. Katy thought of all the other times she had stood here: when she had a problem, or just wanted to be alone. It seemed to calm her – enable her to think rationally, and work things out. 'I'll have to look after Dad today,' she thought. Whilst Katy stood there taking in the view, her mind wandered back to her wedding-dress hanging in her bedroom. Today should have been the happiest day of her life, but one person would be missing. Her mother would only be with her in spirit: Katy's mum had died suddenly, six weeks before - the day after completing Katy's dress – such a shock. The resulting funeral had been very emotional - more so, because of the forthcoming wedding. Jim, having returned unnoticed, nudged her hand – he always instinctively knew when she was sad. She stroked his soft coat: he was such a comfort.

"Come on, Jim, we have a wedding to attend," she said, pulling herself together. "Mum wouldn't have wanted us to be sad today. You will look after Mum, won't you, Jim?" Jim would be at the wedding too, because the church was only a few yards from their house. He knew this day was different – something good was happening, and he recognised the name 'Mum'. But he didn't understand why Katy had asked him to look after Mum on that particular day especially, because he looked after her every day: he had to - after all, he was the only one who could see her.

***

# WAITING

WILLIAM SAT IN THE SITTING ROOM, gazing intently through the window - he was going to see his dad today. William was three years old, and his dad had promised to take him to the new park that had opened about a mile from William's home. Apparently, there was an enormous slide, swings, climbing-bars, etc.

His dad didn't live with his wife and young son any more. William didn't really understand, but he did know there had been rows, and long silences. He had heard his parents arguing from his bedroom, when they thought he was asleep. His dad had moved out a few weeks before, but tried to see William every weekend. The problem was, for the last two weekends he'd been unable to keep his promise – the first weekend, his car had broken down, and the following one, he'd caught a tummy-bug, and certainly didn't want to pass it on to his son. He hated letting him down, but sometimes, it wasn't meant to be.

So William was hoping against hope, his dad would turn up this time. He wasn't due until two o'clock, but William had insisted he sit by the window, even though it was only half-past one. He wanted to be sure he'd see his dad's car as soon as it turned into the Close.

"He's not here yet, Mummy!" shouted William. His mum smiled - she hoped he wouldn't be disappointed again. It was she who had to cope with the tears and difficult behaviour, should her husband not arrive. William had been inconsolable last weekend - he'd cried himself to sleep.

She hadn't given up hope that she and her husband could reconcile their differences, given time. They were always so tired, both working long hours – he, as a teacher, and she, as a classroom assistant. William attended a nursery he loved, while his mum was at work. The arguments had been about the usual things – money: they were still trying to pay off the mortgage; housework was a constant battle – who would do what, and when. They seemed such silly reasons to row about, when she thought about it. If only they could afford a holiday – it would recharge their batteries, and give them some quality time together, as a family, and William would love it.

"He's here!" William's shout interrupted her thoughts. 'Thank goodness!' She heaved a sigh of relief. William ran to open the door, as his dad walked up the path. The sight of her husband took her breath away – she still loved him. He smiled, and lifted his son up in his strong arms – he loved his William so much.

"When you bring William back, would you like to stay for tea?" she suggested.

"I'd love to," he replied – things were looking up. Perhaps they could rekindle what they once had – he had never stopped loving her – he still wasn't sure why he'd decided to move out. They would have to take things slowly, but he was suddenly optimistic.

As father and son walked down the path towards the car, they turned to wave. She started planning what to make for tea – something special perhaps. She began to feel excited – William would be so happy if his dad moved back in, and it would make things so much easier. For the first time in weeks she began to look forward to the future. Perhaps the happy family unit she'd always dreamed of was on the horizon.

# THE ULTIMATE GIFT

As Jane got off the bus, she couldn't stop smiling. Some people reciprocated her smile; others looked at her strangely. 'Perhaps they think I'm a bit odd,' thought Jane, but she didn't care. She was on her way home from the doctor's, having had her second pregnancy confirmed.

Her son Michael was three years old, and attending Nursery, so this would be the perfect time to have another baby. She remembered Michael's birth very well – she'd had an epidural, so it had been relatively pain-free. What she hadn't been prepared for was the unrelenting tiredness that plagued her for what seemed like months following the birth. She really wasn't confident looking after a new baby – it was simply trial and error. Nothing had prepared her for this. The nurses at the hospital hadn't helped, saying things like – "You can't breast-, and bottle-feed!"

'Why not?' thought Jane. This was complete nonsense, of course: she knew that now, and couldn't understand how they got away with advising such rubbish. She'd asked them if they'd had children – they confessed they hadn't. Jane thought *that* said it all. But a second baby would be very different – Jane would know exactly what to do, and when. 'This time it'll be a doddle,' she thought.

It was too early to collect Michael, so she sat down on a park bench, deep in thought. She could think of nothing else but her excitement over her forthcoming baby. Suddenly, she remembered Rachel - how could she have forgotten? Rachel, a very close friend, and husband Ray, had been trying for a baby for five years, with little success. Rachel had suffered two miscarriages, which had almost ruined their marriage. They'd had all the tests, and had now resorted to 'IVF' (in vitro fertilization). This was a painful, heart-breaking process, which might, or might not, be successful. Jane's heart went out to them – life could be so unfair at times. Jane had no trouble at all getting pregnant – she supposed she was lucky. But that didn't stop her from feeling very guilty when she thought of her friend. Then, like a bolt from the blue, Jane had an idea. Then, almost as quickly, she dismissed it. 'I can't,' she thought. Then, 'Why not?'

Jane's idea was surrogacy. When she'd had her next baby, her family would be complete. She had never wanted more than two children. She could have a baby for Rachel and Ray, couldn't she? She'd have to discuss it with her husband Richard, of course, but was hopeful he'd agree.

Jane looked at her watch – it was time to collect Michael. She walked the few yards to the Nursery. Michael ran to greet her, clutching a sheet of paper - a collage of a daffodil – it was the first of March – St. David's Day. He showed it to her proudly.

"It's beautiful, Michael. Did you make this yourself?" she asked. Michael nodded, smiling.

"With a little help," said Margaret, who ran the Nursery. "See you tomorrow Michael."

Walking home, Michael chatted about what he'd done that day. Jane thought how lucky she was. She'd run her idea past Richard that night, although she knew what he'd say – 'Let's get this pregnancy over with first, and if there are no complications, then you can think seriously about surrogacy. There might be no need, though - the IVF might work.' It would be wonderful - thought Jane - to actually have a baby for someone: it would be the ultimate gift.

# HOPE

THE VERY FIRST TIME Eleri felt her baby move inside her, she was at the supermarket checkout. She stopped loading the conveyer belt, a fresh-looking spring cabbage in her hand. She wondered whether she'd imagined it, but no, there it was again. The feeling was so tentative, gentle - like a butterfly - it was hardly noticeable.

"Are you ok?" asked the lady behind her.

"Yes, sorry," replied Eleri, and hurriedly put the remaining groceries on the conveyor. She couldn't wait to get out of the queue so she could text her husband Alex. She knew he'd be as thrilled as she was.

Driving home, her thoughts returned to the many disappointments they'd endured as a couple – three miscarriages (the worst times in their lives) and finally - IVF. It had worked first time, thankfully. It could be an expensive business.

Her thoughts returned to the day she realised she was pregnant after IVF – she was ecstatic. The first three months were a nightmare though – she was so afraid of losing this baby too. But after her three month scan, she relaxed a little. And now, at five months, her baby was moving - it was reassuring. Surely nothing would go wrong now? The thought was unbearable. 'Think of something positive,' she scolded herself.

She arrived home, and put her shopping away. 'I'll be sensible, and put my feet up,' she thought. She put the kettle on, made a cup of tea, and switched on the television, but she couldn't find anything of interest to watch. She switched it off.

The next day, she was having her twenty-week scan – she was looking forward to it, but was apprehensive too. Alex was taking the morning off work to accompany her. They'd been told they could find out the sex of their baby at this scan, but they'd decided not to. As long as the baby was healthy, they didn't mind whether it was a boy, or a girl.

The following morning, Eleri and Alex drove to the hospital. It was a beautiful Spring morning – the type of morning that made you feel good to be alive. The hedgerows were alive with flowers – primroses, bluebells and violets nestled in the green grass. Eleri thought it was early for violets, but then, miracles of nature did happen, and always took her by surprise: much like her baby – which was indeed a miracle, with a little medical intervention - of course.

They reached the hospital, and sat in a beautiful room to await Julia, the midwife – she was always running late, because she cared and took time with her patients. Eleri didn't mind – the waiting room was lovely – the sun's rays were streaming in through the window, dancing against the oval mirror on the other side of the room. The carpet was a nice shade of red – not garish. And the cushioned chairs were a combination of black and red, with gold trim. Eleri noticed a black cat, curled up on a red cushion, on a chair, near the window. Now that was unusual, thought Eleri, but it added to the ambience. The cat suddenly looked up at Eleri, and winked!

"Eleri Williams." Eleri jumped, she had been so engrossed with the cat, she hadn't noticed Julia putting her head around the door.

"Yes," replied Eleri. She looked back at the cat, which was now washing his face with his paw. Eleri shook her head, and rose carefully to accompany Alex into the consulting-room.

"How have you been?" asked Julia.

"Fine," answered Eleri. "I felt the baby move yesterday."

"Fantastic," said Julia. "Let's see what the scan tells us."

Eleri waited excitedly, with some trepidation, while Julia moved the probe over her tummy. There was her baby – he/she moved quickly – disturbed by the probe being pressed on his mother's tummy, no doubt.

"The heart is beating strongly," said Julia, "Would you like to know the sex of your baby?"

"No," Eleri and Alex replied in unison. "We'd prefer it to be a surprise."

"Yes, most couples do," Julia smiled. She moved the probe around – the picture was amazingly clear. "Well, as far as I can see, everything looks completely normal, and your baby is a good size. We'll book you in for your next scan, but I don't foresee any problems whatsoever." After some routine questions, Eleri and Alex thanked Julia, and walked out of the consulting room.

As they passed the waiting room, Eleri looked in, but the cat had gone. They walked out into the warm sunshine. Eleri saw the cat immediately – he was waiting for them, and approached, meowing and purring. He wound himself around Eleri's legs; she bent down to stroke him.

"You are so friendly," murmured Eleri. "I wish I could take you home." The cat was suddenly distracted by a rustle in the grass, and crossed the path in front of Eleri and Alex - in search of a mouse, no doubt.

"Well," said Alex, "That's a good omen, if ever I saw one." Eleri smiled - things were going to work out just fine this time, and they both walked happily, hand in hand, towards their waiting car.